I got a CROCODILE

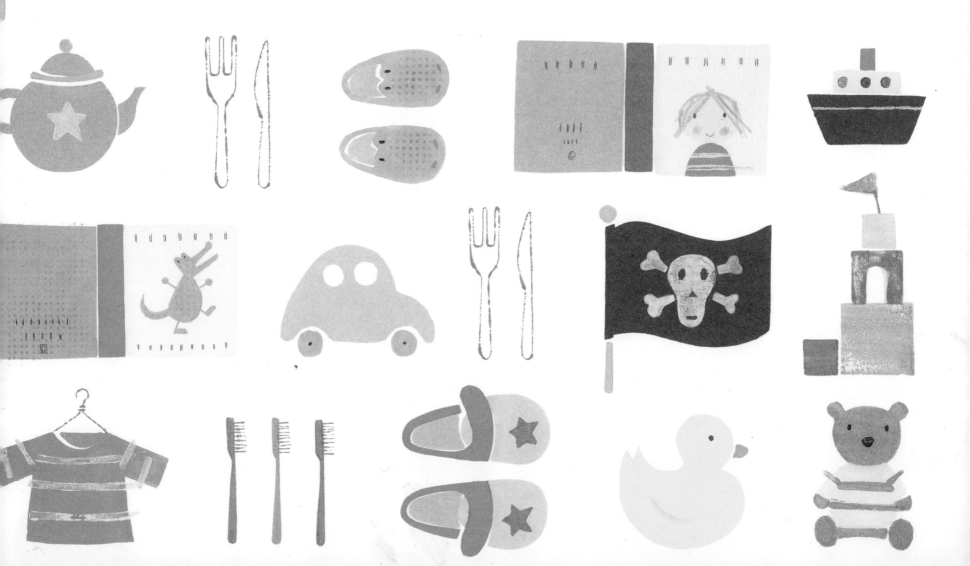

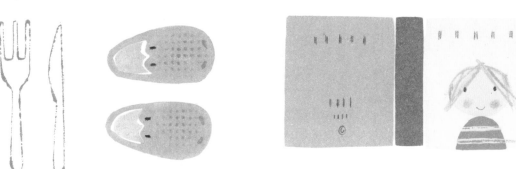

For my family: Mum, Dad, Rick, Laura and Sheels

★ ★ ★

SIMON AND SCHUSTER

First published in Great Britain in 2013 by Simon and Schuster UK Ltd 1st Floor, 222 Gray's Inn Road, London WC1X 8HB A CBS Company

Text and illustrations copyright © 2013 Nicola Killen

978-0-85707-577-2 (HB)
978-0-85707-578-9 (PB)
978-0-85707-895-7 (eBook)

Printed in China
10 9 8 7 6 5 4 3 2 1

I got a CROCODILE

SIMON AND SCHUSTER
London New York Sydney Toronto New Delhi

Nicola Killen

I always wanted a brother or sister...

...but instead I got a crocodile.

It was quite a surprise!

At first I liked having Crocodile around.

But then...

there was terrible trouble
at teatime.

Big bother
at bathtime.

And bedtime was no better.

Everywhere I went
Crocodile followed,

and followed

and followed,

and FOLLOWED!

"GO AWAY!"

I always knew when Crocodile
was sad because he cried,
and cried,

and cried

and CRIED!

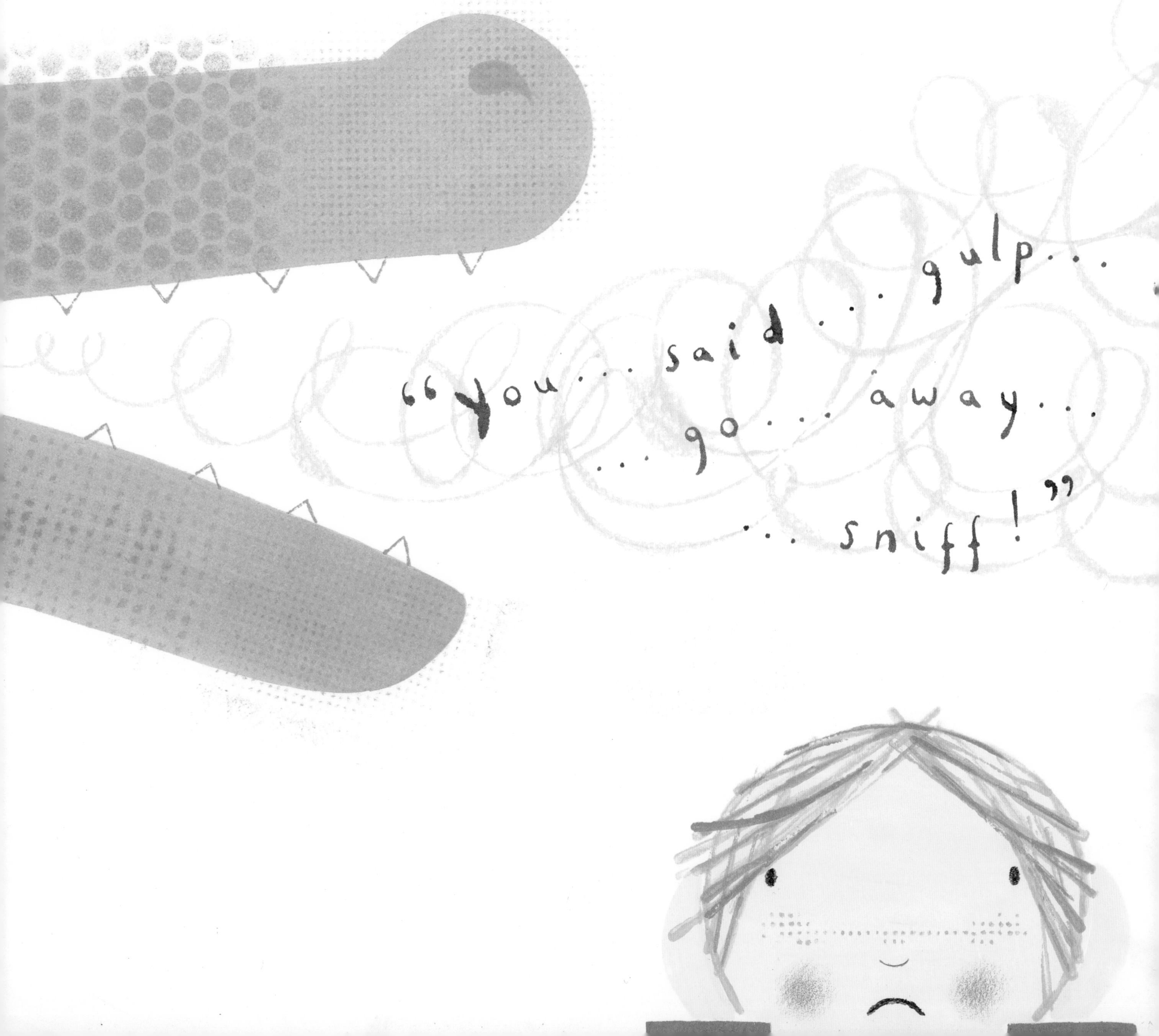
"You . . . said . . . gulp . . .
go . . . away . . .
. . . sniff!"

But nobody could tell when I was sad...

...except Crocodile!

So we became friends again,

and started having fun together!

Who else could be
my royal dragon?

Or my big, green slide?

Or my pirate island?

Now we get on REALLY well together.

There's never trouble at teatime.

No bother at bathtime.

And bedtime is a breeze.

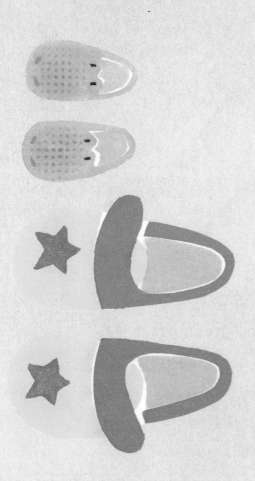

I always wanted
a brother or sister...

...but I'm glad I got my crocodile instead!